DRUMHELLER DINOSAUR DANCE

Written by

Robert Heidbreder

Illustrated by

Bill Slavin and
Esperança Melo

Kids Can Press

Drumheller dinosaurs lie around,
bones buried deep in ancient ground.

Dry bones rest in dusty sleep – skulls, claws,

Drumheller dinosaurs make no

jaws down dinosaur deep.

noise. All day they're as silent as dinosaur toys.

But when the moon rises in the sky,
Drumheller dinosaurs transmogrify.

They stir their bones from secret cracks
and assemble themselves —
fronts, sides and backs.

Drumheller dinosaurs rise up tall.
Across the Badlands they skeleton-crawl.

They creep to a spot that they all know.
They band together, ROAR

They grab buried drums and begin a beat. They

BOOMITY-BOOM   RATTELY-CLACK

rattle, clack, stomp on dinosaur feet.

THUMPITY-THUMP WHICKETY-WHACK

Cymbals crash, stone castanets snap.
They dance back to life with a clickity-clap.

They tango,
fandango and break-dance with ease.
They whirl on

BOOMITY-BOOM   RATTELY-CLACK

their tails and twirl on their knees.

THUMPITY-THUMP WHICKETY-WHACK

With wild tambourines they shimmy and shake.
They rock and they roll – it's a dino earthquake!

BOOMITY-BOOM RATTELY-CLACK

THUMPITY-THUMP

WHICKETY-WHACK

The thunderous beat rolls into town.

Sleep is disturbed for miles around.

"A terrible storm!"
the grown-ups shout.
But the kids all know that the dinos are out.

The dinosaurs' party is loud and long,

BOOMITY-BOOM RATTELY-CLACK

with drumming and dancing and Drumheller song.

THUMPITY-THUMP WHICKETY-WHACK

The kids go to sleep to the dinosaur beat.
They bob their heads and tip-tap their feet.

They dance in their dreams
with wiggles and jiggles,
Smiles on their faces and mouths full of giggles.

But when dark night gives way to the day,
Drumheller dinosaurs stash drums away.

Then off they clatter through dinosaur land,

BOOMITY-BOOM RATTELY-CLACK

keeping the beat of their Drumheller band.

THUMPITY-THUMP   WHICKETY-WHACK

Across the Badlands they creep to their beds,
unsnap tired bones and bury sleepy heads.

They're deep in the earth
by dawn's first light,

where they wait all day long
for dinosaur night.

To my five grandnieces, with love — R.H.

For Mia, who loves to dance on the wild side — B.S. & E.M.

Many thanks to the Royal Tyrrell Museum and Eric Snively, M.Sc., University of Calgary,
for their generous help in identifying the Drumheller dinosaurs.

Drumheller, Alberta, Canada, is one of the best places on Earth to find dinosaur bones, and it is home to the world-famous Royal Tyrrell Museum. There are 350–400 known ancient dinosaur species in the world, and over 60 are from Alberta! Some of these Drumheller dinosaurs are featured in this book.

Kids Can Press acknowledges the financial support of the Government of Ontario, through the Ontario Media Development Corporation's Ontario Book Initiative; the Ontario Arts Council; the Canada Council for the Arts; and the Government of Canada, through the CBF, for our publishing activity.

Published in Canada by
Kids Can Press Ltd.
25 Dockside Drive
Toronto, ON M5A 0B5

Published in the U.S. by
Kids Can Press Ltd.
2250 Military Road
Tonawanda, NY 14150

www.kidscanpress.com

The artwork in this book was rendered in acrylics, on gessoed paper
The text is set in Alleycat

Edited by Tara Walker
Designed by Bill Slavin and Esperança Melo

The hardcover edition of this book is smyth sewn casebound.
The paperback edition of this book is limp sewn with a drawn-on cover.
Manufactured in Tseung Kwan O, NT Hong Kong, China, in 12/2014 by Paramount Printing Co. Ltd.

CM 04 0 9 8 7 6 5 4 3
CM PA 06 0 9 8 7

Library and Archives Canada Cataloguing in Publication

Heidbreder, Robert
Drumheller dinosaur dance / written by Robert Heidbreder ; illustrated by Bill Slavin and Esperança Melo

ISBN 978-1-55337-393-3 (bound) ISBN 978-1-55337-982-9 (pbk.)

I. Slavin, Bill II. Melo, Esperança III. Title.

PS8565.E42D78 2004   jC813'.54   C2003-906536-7

Kids Can Press is a **corus**™ Entertainment company